GET OFF MY L...

MICHAEL GARLAND

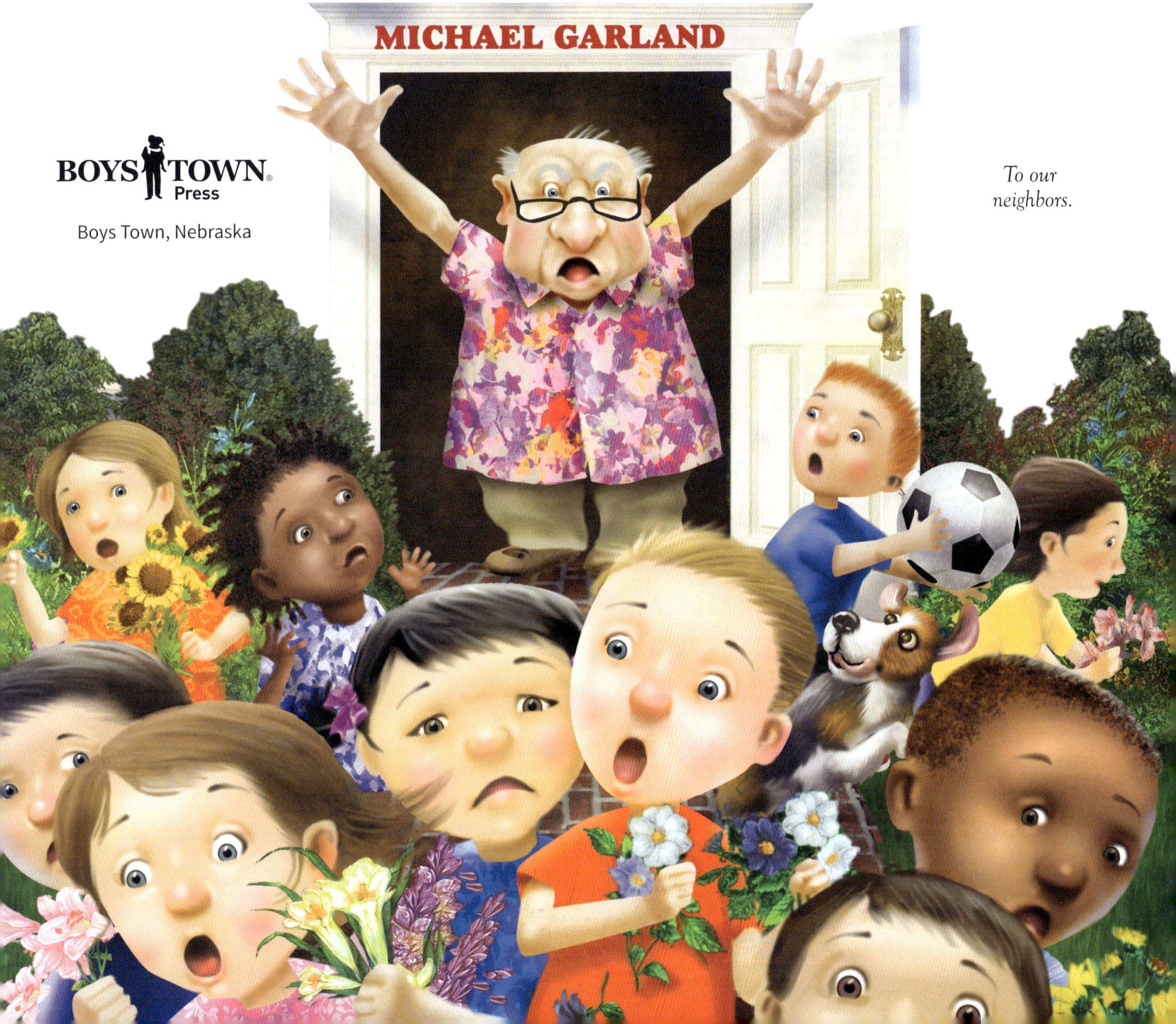

BOYS TOWN Press

Boys Town, Nebraska

To our neighbors.

Get Off My Lawn!

Text and Illustrations Copyright © 2021 by Father Flanagan's Boys' Home
ISBN 978-1-944882-75-4

Published by the Boys Town Press, 13603 Flanagan Blvd., Boys Town, NE 68010

All rights reserved under International and Pan-American Copyright Conventions. Unless otherwise noted, no part of this book may be reproduced, stored in a retrieval system, or transmitted in any form or by any means, electronic, mechanical, photocopying, recording, or otherwise, without express written permission of the publisher, except for brief quotations or critical reviews.

For a Boys Town Press catalog, call **1-800-282-6657**
or visit our website: **BoysTownPress.org**

Publisher's Cataloging-in-Publication Data

Names: Garland, Michael, 1952- author.

Title: Get off my lawn! / Michael Garland.

Description: Boys Town, NE : Boys Town Press, [2021] | Audience: ages 2-8; grades pre-K to 4. | Summary: Mr. Smith's pride and joy are his colorful flowers and perfectly manicured lawn. So, when he eyes the neighborhood kids traipsing through his yard and trampling his flowers, he roars "Get off my lawn!" The kids think he's mean for ruining their fun, but one mom knows exactly where the blame belongs. Follow along as the children learn why they need to make amends for their behavior.–Publisher.

Identifiers: ISBN: 978-1-944882-75-4

Subjects: LCSH: Courtesy–Juvenile fiction. | Respect–Juvenile fiction. | Lawns–Juvenile fiction. | Gardens–Juvenile fiction. | Emotions–Juvenile fiction. | Peer pressure in children–Juvenile fiction. | Social values–Juvenile fiction. | Child psychology–Juvenile fiction. | Children–Life skills guides–Juvenile fiction. | CYAC: Etiquette–Fiction. | Respect–Fiction. | Lawns– Fiction. | Gardens–Fiction. | Emotions–Fiction. | Peer pressure–Fiction. | Social values– Fiction. | Behavior–Fiction. | Conduct of life–Fiction. | BISAC: JUVENILE FICTION / Social Themes / Manners & Etiquette. | JUVENILE FICTION / Social Themes / Emotions & Feelings. | JUVENILE FICTION / Social Themes / Peer Pressure. | JUVENILE FICTION / Social Themes / Values & Virtues. | EDUCATION / Early Childhood.

Classification: LCC: PZ7.G3734 G47 2021 | DDC: [E]–dc23

 Boys Town Press is the publishing division of Boys Town, a national organization serving children and families.

Printed in the United States
10 9 8 7 6 5 4 3 2 1

Sun and shade.

Grass and flowers.

"Let's play!"

Pink flowers.
Yellow flowers.
Purple flowers.

Blue flowers.

Orange flowers.

Red flowers.

"What?"

"On his lawn."

"You're not supposed to play on Mr. Smith's lawn. He works so hard on his beautiful yard, and it's very rude to go on someone's property without permission."

"You should tell Mr. Smith that you're sorry."

"We're afraid to go back there."

"Maybe you could do something nice for him."

"Like what?"

"We're sorry! We know we shouldn't have ruined your flowers. We made these for you. And can we help you clean up?"

"Well, after we clean up the yard, maybe I can find a spot for you kids to play – if you ask permission first."

Always think about how the things you do will affect others. Treat other people the way you would like to be treated – with kindness and respect. If you do something wrong, say you're sorry.

TIPs for Parents & Educators

It's natural for young children to get excited and then behave in ways that might seem rude. Teaching children how to look at situations from the point of view of others, or to have empathy, is one way to help kids better understand how their behaviors can affect those around them.

For many children, however, empathy and perspective-taking are challenging concepts to grasp. You can help build empathy and perspective-taking in children by teaching the Boys Town Social Skills of "Asking Permission" and "Making an Apology."

When kids learn how to ask permission, it encourages them to think before they act and avoid the missteps that can get them into trouble.

To teach the skill of **"Asking Permission,"** have kids practice these behavioral steps:

1. Look at the person.
2. Use a nice voice.
3. Say "May I... please?"
4. Accept the answer calmly.*

*Young children may need extra guidance and help from you to understand what it looks like to accept an answer calmly, especially when the answer is no.

Asking permission won't automatically prevent bad choices or behavioral mistakes. So when mistakes happen, children need to know how to apologize.

To teach the skill of **"Making an Apology,"** have kids practice these behavioral steps:

1. Look at the person.
2. Use a calm voice and show that you mean it.
3. Say "I'm sorry for..."
4. Say "Next time, I'll try to... " or "I'll try not to..."

BOYS TOWN
Saving Children Healing Families

For more parenting information, visit boystown.org/parenting.

Boys Town Press books
Kid-friendly books for teaching social skills

The *Socially Skilled Kids* book series gives children the know-how and courage to overcome their fears, learn essential social skills and have healthier, happier relationships.

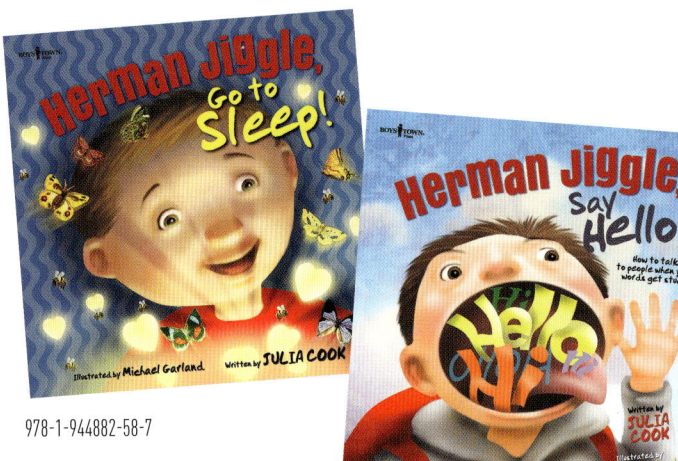

978-1-944882-58-7

978-1-944882-51-8

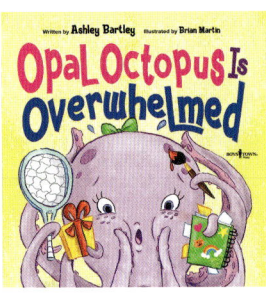

978-1-944882-73-0

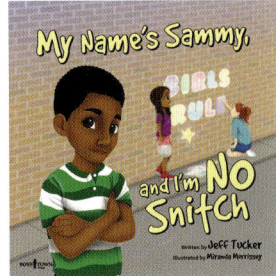

978-1-944882-61-7

A book series to help kids master social situations.

Downloadable Activities
Go to BoysTownPress.org to download.

978-1-944882-42-6

978-1-944882-54-9

978-1-944882-69-3

OTHER TITLES:
Freddie the Fly: Motormouth;
Freddie the Fly: Connecting the Dots; Freddie the Fly: Bee On, Buzz Off

978-1-944882-18-1

For information on Boys Town and its Education Model, Common Sense Parenting®, and training programs:
boystowntraining.org | boystown.org/parenting
training@BoysTown.org | 1-800-545-5771

For parenting and educational books and other resources:
BoysTownPress.org
btpress@BoysTown.org | 1-800-282-6657